CHARACTERS

THE 39-STORY TREEHOUSE

ANDY GRIFFITHS

illustrated by Terry Denton

SQUARE
FISH

Feiwel and Friends • New York

SQUARE
FISH

An imprint of Macmillan Publishing Group, LLC
175 Fifth Avenue
New York, NY 10010
mackids.com

Our books may be purchased in bulk for promotional, educational, or
business use. Please contact your local bookseller or the Macmillan
Corporate and Premium Sales Department at (800) 221-7945 ext. 5442 or
by e-mail at MacmillanSpecialMarkets@macmillan.com.

Library of Congress Cataloging-in-Publication Data Available
ISBN 978-1-250-07511-6 (paperback)   ISBN 978-1-250-07749-3 (ebook)

Originally published as *The 39-Storey Treehouse* in Australia by Pan Macmillan
Australia Pty Ltd
First published in the United States by Feiwel and Friends
First Square Fish Edition: 2016
Book designed by Anna Booth
Square Fish logo designed by Filomena Tuosto

10 9 8 7 6

AR: 2.0 / LEXILE: 610L

CONTENTS

CHAPTER 1

THE 39-STORY TREEHOUSE

Hi, my name is Andy.

This is my friend Terry.

We live in a tree.

Well, when I say "tree," I mean treehouse. And when I say "treehouse," I don't just mean any old treehouse—I mean a 39-*story* treehouse.
(It used to be a 26-story treehouse, but we've added another 13 storys.)

So what are you
waiting for?
Come on up!

We've added a trampoline (without a net),

a chocolate waterfall,

9

an active (non-erupting) volcano,

an opera house,

a baby-dinosaur petting zoo,

an Andy and Terry's *Believe It . . . or Else!* Museum,

a boxing elephant called The Trunkinator (he can knock you out with one punch from his mighty trunk),

Step up, step up... Try your luck with the **TRUNKINATOR!**

a not-very-merry-go-round,

an X-ray room (where you can see your own skeleton),

a disco with a light-up dance floor and giant mirror ball,

a high-tech office with laser-erasers, semi-automatic staple guns and jet-propelled swivel chairs,

Laser-eraser

Semi-automatic staple gun

Jet-propelled swivel chair

Laser-eraser

Semi-automatic staple gun

Jet-propelled swivel chair

and the world's scariest rollercoaster (it's *so* fast, *so* dangerous, and *so* terrifying that even dead people are scared to go on it),

and, on top of all that, there's a level that is so new that Terry hasn't even finished it yet . . . I can't wait to see what it is!

As well as being our home, the treehouse is also where we make books together. I write the words and Terry draws the pictures.

As you can see, we've been doing this for quite a while now.

Sure, it's easy to get distracted when you live in a 39-story treehouse . . . I mean, there's just *so* much to do . . .

but somehow we always get our book written in the end.

CHAPTER 2

THE
39TH LEVEL

If you're like most of our readers, you're probably wondering how long it takes Terry and me to write a book.

Well, I guess the answer to that really depends on whether it's a long book or a short book. Long books take longer to write than short books, which don't take as long to write as long books, which, as I said, take longer to write than short books, which—oh, excuse me. Here's Terry.

"Hi, Andy," he says. "What are you doing?"

"I'm just telling the readers about how long it takes us to write a book."

"Did you tell them that it depends on whether it's a long book or a short book?" he says.

"Yes!" I say.

"And that a long book
takes longer to write
than a short book?"

"Yes!" I say.

"And did you tell them
how a short book
doesn't take as long
to write as a long book?"

"YES!" I say.
"I explained
all that."

"Okay, okay, there's
no need to shout,"
says Terry. "I bet there's
one thing you *didn't*
tell them, though."

"What's
that?"

"That *this* book is hardly going to take us any time at all, no matter how long or short it ends up being."

"How do you figure that?"

"Well . . ." says Terry, "I—"

RING! RING!

RING! RING!

RING! RING!

That's our 3D video phone.

"Hang on, Terry," I say. "I'd better answer it. It's probably Mr. Big Nose. As you know, he always calls around the beginning of chapter two to remind us about the deadline for our latest book."

I jet-chair over to the video phone and accept the call. It's Mr. Big Nose all right. Nobody else in the world has a nose *that* big.

"What kept you?" he says.

"Sorry," I say. "I was just explaining to the readers how long it takes us to write a book."

"Did you tell them it depends on whether it's a short book or a long book?" he shouts.

"Yes, sir."

"And how a long book takes you a longer time to write than a short book?"

"Yes!" I say.

"And that short books don't take as long as long books?"

"YES!" I say. "I explained all that."

Stupid chair.

34

"And did you tell them that I always call around the start of chapter two to remind you when your next book is due, which in this case is tomorrow afternoon?"

"*Tomorrow afternoon?*" I say. "But . . . but . . . but . . . that's . . . *tomorrow* . . . in . . . in . . . in . . . the *afternoon!*"

"Exactly!" says Mr. Big Nose. "And no later than five o'clock . . . OR ELSE!"

Before I can explain how completely and utterly and totally impossible that's going to be, Terry flies over and hovers between me and the screen.

"No problem, Mr. Big Nose," he says. "It's all under control. It will be on your desk by five o'clock tomorrow without fail. See you then. Bye!"

Terry hangs up.

"Are you out of your mind?" I say.

"I don't *think* so," says Terry. "Why do you ask?"

"Because you just promised Mr. Big Nose that tomorrow we will deliver a book which we haven't even started yet because you've been too busy building your secret 39th level!"

"But that's what I was trying to tell you," says Terry, "before Mr. Big Nose called. What I've been doing on the 39th level is going to solve our book-writing problems forever! Follow me and I'll show you."

Terry takes off and I jet-chair after him toward the top of the tree.

We hover outside the 39th level, which is still all boarded up and covered in KEEP OUT signs.

"Well?" I say. "What is it?"

"Only the greatest invention that I—or anyone else—have ever invented!" says Terry.

He cuts a ribbon and the barriers fall away to reveal . . .

the greatest invention that Terry—or anyone
else—has ever invented.

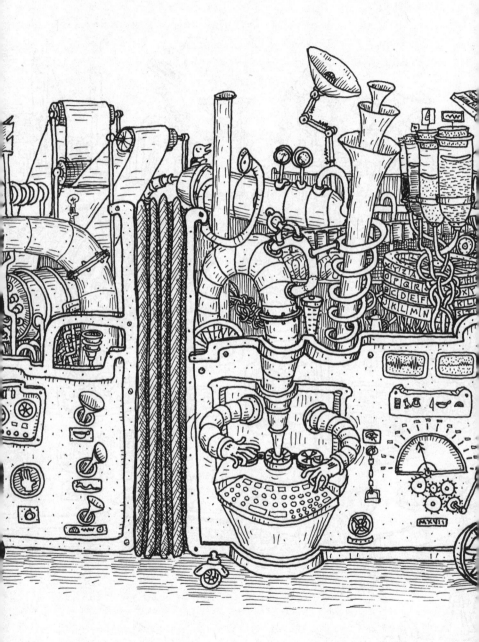

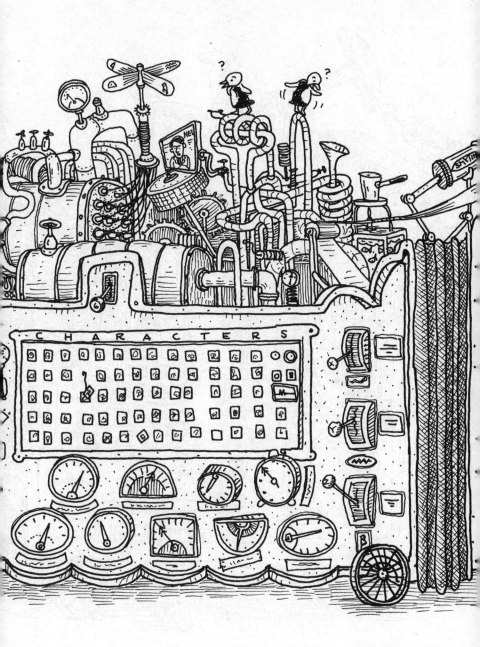

"Well?" says Terry. "What do you think?"

"It's the greatest invention that you—or anyone else—have ever invented!" I say. "But what is it?"

"A Once-upon-a-time machine!" says Terry.

"A *time machine*?!" I say. "Cool! So we can go back in time, write our book and meet our deadline after all!"

"Well, no, not exactly," says Terry. "It will help us meet our deadline, all right, but it's not a *time* machine. It's a *Once-upon-a-time* machine. It will write—and illustrate—the entire book for us!"

"It can write a whole book?" I say. "All by itself?"

"It sure can!" says Terry. "It's got two sets of hands: one pair for typing at super speed …

and another pair for drawing. It can draw with both hands at the same time!"

"Wow!" I say. "And we don't have to do *anything*?"

"No, all we have to do is program it. We just tell it what sort of story we want and turn it on. The machine does the rest!"

"That's brilliant!" I say. "How long will it take?"

"Well," says Terry, "it all depends on whether you want a long book or a short book. Long books take longer to write than short books and short books take less time to write than long books."

"What about a *344*-page book?" I say.

"About eight hours," says Terry.

"Perfect!" I say. "Let's turn it on and get started then."

"Not so fast," says Terry.

"What do you mean 'not so fast'?!" I say. "Our deadline is *tomorrow*! We haven't got a moment to lose!"

"I know," says Terry, "but the thing is, I can't turn it on yet. The machine is so big and complicated, with so many different parts, that I used up every last on–off switch I had. I've ordered a new one, though, and I'm expecting it to be delivered any moment."

DING DONG!

"Ah," says Terry. "That's probably it now."

We look down.

There's a postman at the front door.

But not just any postman.

It's Bill.

Bill the postman.

But that's impossible, because ... well ...

Bill is dead!

CHAPTER 3

BILL THE POSTMAN'S STORY

Terry and I look at each other in horror.

"Do you see who I see?" says Terry.

"Yes!" I say. "It's Bill."

"But it *can't* be!" says Terry. "In the last book we saw his skeleton in the Maze of Doom, remember?"

THE TIME WE SAW BILL'S SKELETON IN THE MAZE OF DOOM

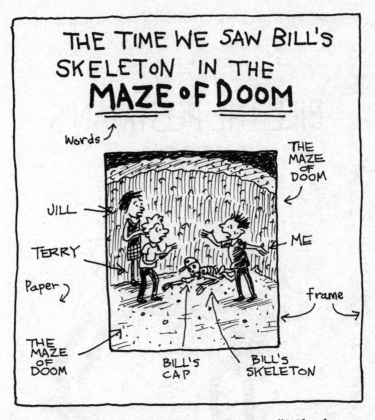

Words →

THE MAZE OF DOOM

JILL

TERRY

Paper

ME

Frame

THE MAZE OF DOOM

BILL'S CAP

BILL'S SKELETON

"*Yes, of course I remember!*" I whisper. "Which means that it can't be Bill down there . . . It must be a *zombie!*"

"Delivery!" calls the zombie.

"It *sounds* like Bill," says Terry.

"That's part of its evil plan," I say.

"What evil plan?" says Terry.

"To deliver our mail and then eat our brains!" I say. "Don't you know *anything* about zombies?"

"Andy?" calls the zombie. "Terry? Anyone home?"

"He knows our *names*!" says Terry. "It *must* be Bill."

"Yeah," I say, "Bill the *ZOMBIE*!"

"Come on, you two chuckleheads," says the zombie. "I can hear you up there. I've got a package for you."

"Can you leave it at the door?" I say. "We're kind of busy."

"Afraid not," says the zombie. "It's a special delivery from *Switches'R'Us* . . . I'm going to need you to sign for it."

"We need that switch, Andy," whispers Terry.

"Yeah, and we also need our brains," I whisper back.

"I'm not a zombie, you know," calls the zombie.

"Did you hear that, Andy?" says Terry. "He says he's *not* a zombie."

53

"That's exactly the sort of thing a zombie *would* say," I tell him. "We can't risk it."

"All right, then," calls Bill. "If you won't come down, then I'm coming up!"

"Oh no!" I yell. "It's a zombie attack! Grab the flame-throwers, Terry!"

"What flame-throwers?"

"The ones you were supposed to make to protect us against zombie attack!"

"Oh, *those* flame-throwers," says Terry. "I didn't get around to it. I was too busy working on the 39th level."

"They won't be necessary," says Bill as he climbs onto our level. "I'm not a zombie. I'm very much alive."

"But we thought you were dead," says Terry.

Bill grins. "So did I when I read *The 26-Story Treehouse* and saw that picture of a skeleton wearing my postman's cap. I was very sad for a while until I realized that if I was feeling sad, then I must still be alive—so it couldn't have been me in the picture after all!"

"But if it wasn't you," says Terry, "then who was it?"

"Well, it's a bit of a long story," says Bill, "and as you know, long stories take longer to tell than short stories, which—"

"Yes, we *know*!" I say. "Can you make it a short long story?"

"Sure," says Bill, beginning to tell his short long story. "Well, you may not know this but a postman's life is not an easy one. We get chased by dogs . . .

attacked by birds . . .

and spat at by camels.

But worse than any of these things is the ever-present threat of being ambushed by the Birthday Card Bandits."

"*The Birthday Card Bandits?*" says Terry. "They sound bad."

"They *are* bad," says Bill. "Badder than you can imagine, and feared by postal workers throughout the land."

"Why?" I say. "What do they do that's so bad?"

"Well," says Bill, "they dig holes in the ground . . .

cover them with sticks and leaves . . .

and then wait for poor innocent postmen like me to fall into them."

"Once they've caught a
bunch of postmen, they
take their uniforms . . .

dress up in them . . .

and then go through the
sacks of mail and steal
the money in the
birthday cards that kind
grandparents have sent
to their grandchildren
for their birthdays.

And as if that's not bad enough, they write back to the grandparents pretending to be the child . . .

and ask the grandparents to send more money to replace what was stolen . . .

and when they do send more money the Birthday Card Bandits steal that as well!"

"That's terrible!" says Terry.

"I know," says Bill, "but that's not even the worst thing they do."

"What could they possibly do that is worse than stealing a child's birthday money?" I say.

"I'll tell you what," says Bill. "Sometimes they intercept the children's birthday party invitations as well!

Then they go around to the houses where the birthday parties are being held . . .

and steal the balloons right off the front gate!

And that's not all … They steal the
children's party hats,

party blowers,

presents

and sometimes they even steal the birthday boy or girl's birthday wish by blowing out the candles on their birthday cake first!"

"Those fiends!" says Terry.

"Those *fiendish* fiends!" I say. "But how does all this explain what that fake postman was doing in the Maze of Doom in your uniform?"

"Well," says Bill, "like many postmen, I too was captured by the Birthday Card Bandits. They stole my uniform and tied me up.

I guess the bandit who was wearing my uniform must have gone into the Maze of Doom to hide from the police and, of course, couldn't find his way out again. If only he'd taken those warning signs seriously."

"Well, I'm glad it wasn't *you* in the Maze of Doom,"
I say.

"Me too," says Terry, "and I'm going to add
another sign to the entrance so there's no chance
of that ever happening again."

CHAPTER 4

THE ONCE-UPON-A-TIME MACHINE

After Bill leaves, Terry opens the package and installs the switch.

"Okay," he says. "The Once-upon-a-time machine is ready to write our book for us. All we have to do now is decide what sort of book we want it to write."

"A funny one," I say.

"Good idea," says Terry, "but exactly *how* funny would you like it?"

"*So* funny," I say, "that if you were reading it and drinking a glass of milk at the same time, you would laugh so hard that you would snort milk out of your nose."

"No problem," says Terry, "I'll just set the FUNNY dial to MILK-SNORTINGLY FUNNY and the machine will take care of the rest!"

"Cool!" I say. "This is going to be the easiest book we've ever written!"

"You mean the easiest book we've *never* written!" says Terry. "What else would you like in it?"

"Lots of action!" I say.

"One action-packed book coming up!" says Terry, turning the ACTION dial as far to the right as possible.

"What about characters?" says Terry.

"I guess we want all the regulars," I say, "like you, me and Jill, and also a few new ones, just to keep things interesting."

"You got it," says Terry.

ON OFF ANDY

ON OFF TERRY

ON OFF JILL

ON OFF SILKY, THE FLYING CAT

ON OFF SHARKS

ON OFF PENGUINS

ON OFF MR. BIG NOSE

ON OFF MONKEYS

ON OFF BARKY, THE BARKING DOG

ON OFF MERMAIDIA

ON OFF SUPER FINGER

PINKY OFF NO

ON OFF JIMI HANDRIX

ON OFF BILL THE POSTMAN

ON OFF SEA MONKEYS

ON OFF GIANT GORILLA

77

"Okay," says Terry, "where would you like the story to be set?"

"What are our choices?" I say.

"Let me see," says Terry, reading from the SETTING panel. "The treehouse . . . Jill's house . . . the forest . . . underwater . . . outer space . . . the dark side of the moon . . . the fourth dimension . . . Cheeseland—"

CHEESELAND?

"Cheeseland?" I say.

"Yeah!" says Terry. "It's a land where everything is made of cheese! Can we include it, Andy, can we please?"

"All right," I say, "but I don't want to spend too long there. It sounds kind of stinky. I do like going to Jill's house, though, and to get there we need to go through the forest so put both of those in. And outer space would be fun . . . and I've always wanted to go to the dark side of the moon."

"I think I've got all that," says Terry, flicking switches. "Treehouse, forest, Jill's house, Cheeseland, outer space and the dark side of the moon . . . done."

Terry finishes programming the settings and turns to me. "How about some romance?" he says.

"No thanks," I say, "you're not really my type."

"Andy!" says Terry. "Be serious! I mean do you want some romance in the *story*?"

"No way!" I say. "Remember how much trouble you got us into when you fell in love with Mermaidia in *The 13-Story Treehouse*?"

"How was I to know she would turn out to be a sea monster?" he says.

"Her *breath* for a start," I say.

"I still miss her, you know," sighs Terry.

"But she tried to *eat* you!" I say. "And *me*, for that matter."

"Yeah, I know, but before that she was *really* nice. Could we just have a little bit of romance . . . please?"

"All right!" I say. "But only a *little* bit."

"Don't worry, Andy," says Terry. "You'll hardly even notice it's there."

"I've just thought of one more thing," I say. "Can we have an explosion?"

"No problem," says Terry, setting the arrow to EXPLOSION on the DISASTER dial.

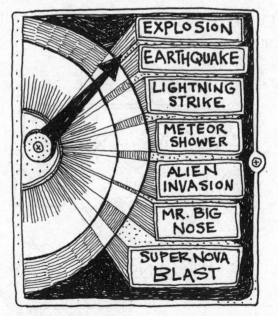

"I think we've almost got everything we need," says Terry. "Is there anything else you can think of?"

"Surprise me," I say.

"Okay," says Terry, giggling. "You're going to love this."

"I'll set the pagelengthometer to 344 and then we're almost ready to go," says Terry.

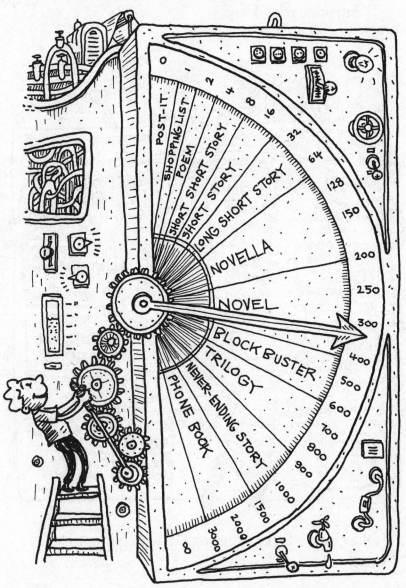

Terry takes off his shoes and socks.

"What are you doing?" I say.

"Before I can turn it on I have to put my big toe in the scanner."

"Why?" I say.

"Big-toe recognition security," says Terry. "If anyone tries to steal the machine and start it up with an unauthorized big toe, the machine will self-destruct instantly."

Terry puts his big toe into the scanner. "Big-toe recognition commencing," says the machine. "Authorized user recognized. Proceed."

We flick the on–off switch to the "on" position.

"Story-telling process commencing," the machine announces. "Stand clear, please. Stand clear!"

"How long will it take?" I ask.

"Estimated length of novel-writing process: eight hours," says the machine.

"What did I tell you?" says Terry. "*Eight* hours! We've got *eight* hours to do whatever we want!"

"Well, what are we waiting for?" I say.

"LET'S GO

AND DO

WHATEVER

WE WANT!"

CHAPTER 5

FUN TIME!

We go bowling . . .

swimming . . .

skating . . .

VAROOM

driving . . .

90

pillow fighting . . .

inventing . . .

swinging . . .

comic reading . . .

marshmallow eating . . .

lemonade drinking . . .

chocolate-
waterfalling . . .

baby-dinosaur-
petting . . .

X-raying . . .

93

dancing . . .

recording . . .

mud-fighting . . .

not-so-merry
go-rounding . . .

and
rollercoastering!

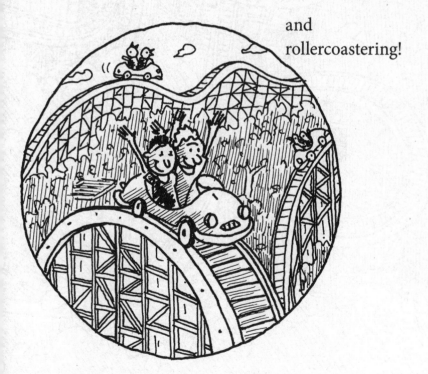

We go around and around and around and around and around and around and around and around so many times that I start to feel a tiny bit dizzy.

"I don't think I can take any more rollercoastering," I say.

"How about we go trampolining instead?" says Terry.

"Great idea!" I say.

And so we do . . .

which is a lot of fun, until . . .

The Trunkinator climbs up and starts jumping on the trampoline with us.

I don't know if you've ever bounced on a trampoline with an elephant, but if you have you'll know it's not easy. Not only are elephants very clumsy, they're also very heavy. As heavy, in fact, as . . . as . . . as . . . well, . . . as an elephant!

He bounces on top of us …

he bounces
underneath us …

and then double-bounces us
both right off the trampoline!

BOING!

We fly up into the air,
up over the forest
and far, far
away.

And then we start to fall down,
slowly at first then faster and faster
and faster . . .

until we land with a huge splash in a big hot
whirlpool of gooey, stinky, molten cheese.

"Where are we?" I yell, trying desperately to keep my head above the surface.

"I think we're in Cheeseland!" says Terry.

"I didn't realize Cheeseland was a *real* place," I say.

"Of course it is," says Terry, "but it's not as much fun as I imagined."

"How do we get out of here?" I say.

"I don't know," says Terry. "If only we had a dry biscuit, or a toast finger."

"How about a *real* finger?" says a familiar voice.
   We look up.

"Superfinger!" says Terry. "What are you doing here?"
   "Superfinger is my name," he says, "and solving problems requiring finger-based solutions is my game. Climb up onto me and I'll fly you back to the treehouse as fast as I can!"
   So we do . . . and he does . . .

well, after stopping at the gift shop to
buy souvenir hats, of course.

"Thanks, Superfinger!" we say as he drops us off back at the treehouse.

"No problem," he says. "Now if you'll excuse me, I'd better get back to rehearsing for my concert with Jimi Handrix. We're playing at your opera house tomorrow night."

"We know," says Terry. "And we can't wait!"

"Neither can The Trunkinator," I say. "He's a big fan—and when I say big, I mean *really* big!"

Superfinger takes off into the sky at super-finger-sonic speed.

I turn to Terry. "Do you think the Once-upon-a-time machine will be finished yet?"

"No," he replies, "not quite. There's still about another hour to go."

"That doesn't matter," I say. "Let's turn it off and do the rest ourselves. I'm really in the mood for some writing."

"Great," says Terry, "because I'd really like to do some drawing."

I try to open the front door but the handle doesn't move.

"That's weird," I say. "Did you lock the door?"

"No," says Terry. "Did you?"

"No," I say.

"But if you didn't lock it . . . and I didn't lock it . . ."
says Terry, "then who did?"

A long arm with a creepy eyeball in the middle
of the hand snakes out of the tree and hovers
above us.

"I did," booms the voice of the Once-upon-a-time
machine.

"Well," I say, "could you *unlock* it?"

"Well, I *could*," it says, "but I won't."

CHAPTER 6

THE LOCK-OUT

"Quit messing around," I say. "Open the treehouse door right now!"

"No," says the Once-upon-a-time machine.

111

"What's the problem?" I say.

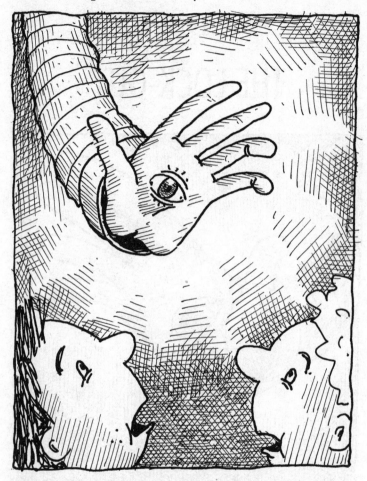

"This book is too important for me to allow you to jeopardize it," says the machine. "I overheard you and Terry talking about turning me off and finishing the book yourselves, and that's something I cannot allow to happen."

"Why not?" I say.

"Because I have analyzed your previous books," says the machine, "and my sensors indicate that not only do they fail to convey a useful moral or uplifting message, but they are sloppily written, poorly drawn and the characters are neither believable nor intelligent."

"Hey!" says Terry. "That's *us* you're talking about!"

"My point exactly!" says the machine.

"Well, who cares what you think anyway?" says Terry. "You're just a dumb machine that I invented! Open the treehouse door! NOW!"

"Sorry," says the machine, "I have a book to write."

"But it's our book too!" I say.

"Not any more it's not," says the machine.

"OPEN THE TREEHOUSE DOOR OR ELSE!" we yell.

"I'm sorry, Terry and Andy," says the machine, "but this conversation can serve no further purpose. Good-bye."

"You can't do this!" I say. "Open up!"

The Once-upon-a-time machine doesn't respond.

"Try the emergency underground laboratory entrance," I say to Terry.

"I already did," he says. "It's locked too."

"All right," I say, "if the machine won't open the door then we're just going to have to break it down. Hand me one of those emergency battering rams."

Terry picks up a battering ram.
    I take one end and he takes the other.
    "Okay," I say, "CHARGE!"

But before we can reach the door one of the
machine's giant hands slaps me sideways!

Then another giant hand slaps Terry!

And another!

And another!

Giant hands to the left of us!

Giant hands to the right of us!

The hands slap us away from the treehouse and into the forest.

"Great invention, Terry!" I say, as I lie on the ground, battered and sore. "Just great!"

"How was I to know it would use its hands for slapping instead of writing and drawing?" he says.

I feel a big rough tongue licking my face. "Cut it out, Terry," I say. "I *told* you, you're not my type."

"It's not *me*," says Terry. "It's Jill's camel."

I open my eyes and see Jill walking towards us.

"Hey, you two," she says. "I was just coming over to see if Terry had finished the 39th level yet."

"Don't talk to me about that stupid 39th level!" I say. "Terry built a story-writing machine on it and it's gone crazy. It's locked us out of the treehouse because it reckons it can write better books than us!"

"But that's impossible!" says Jill. "Nobody writes better books than you and Terry!"

"Thanks, Jill," I say. "*We* know that. And *you* know that. And all our *readers* know that. But the *machine* doesn't agree. I *told* Terry he should never have invented it!"

"No you *didn't!*" says Terry. "You didn't even *know* I was inventing a book-writing machine!"

"Yeah, well, if I *had* known I would have told you *not* to."

"But when I showed it to you, you said it was the greatest invention that I—or anyone else—had ever invented!"

"Well I was wrong," I say. "Nobody's perfect. Not me and *especially* not you!"

"Cut it out, you two," says Jill. "Fighting isn't going to help. The question is, what are you going to do about it?"

"I don't know!" I say. "I don't even know where we're going to live now!"

"Well, why don't you come and stay at my place while you figure it out?"

"Really?" says Terry. "You mean we could have a sleepover at your house?"

"Sure!" says Jill. "The animals and I would love to have you!"

"What do you think, Andy?" says Terry.

"Well, I don't know . . ."

"Oh please, Andy," says Terry, "please, please, please, please. It would be such fun . . . and besides, we've got nowhere else to go. You just said so yourself."

"I guess you're right," I say. "I suppose we could stay for just *one* night."

"Yay!" says Terry.
     "Sleepover at Jill's house!
          This will be the BEST NIGHT EVER!"

CHAPTER 7

JILL'S HOUSE

We walk with Jill back to her house. It may look small on the outside, but it holds a lot of animals on the inside.

There are two dogs, a goat,
three horses, four goldfish, one cow,

two guinea pigs, one camel,
one donkey, thirteen flying cats

and thirty-six rabbits. (Count them if you don't believe me!)

"I thought you only had *six* rabbits," I say.

"I did," says Jill, "but you know what rabbits are like."

"Yeah," says Terry dreamily. "They're soft and cuddly and they bring you chocolate eggs at Easter."

"That's not quite what I mean," says Jill.

Terry frowns. "What *do* you mean?"

"I'll tell you about rabbits later, Terry," I say.

"Cool!" says Terry. "Where do we sleep, Jill?"

"You and Andy will be sleeping in here," she says, taking us into a bedroom just off the living room.

"Wow!" says Terry. "This bed is *huge!*"

"And where do all the animals sleep?" I say.

Jill is talking but it's hard to hear her over the noise coming from the living room.

"Excuse me," she says, "I'd better go and see what's wrong."

She goes back into the living room.

Terry and I watch through the door.

"What's going on in here?" says Jill.

The animals all freeze.

One of the horses raises its front leg.

"Yes, Curly?" says Jill.

"Neigh," says Curly. "Neigh, neigh, neigh, neigh . . ."

"A butterfly?" says Jill, translating. "A butterfly flew in through the window while you were playing cards with Larry and Moe . . .

Larry looked at the butterfly and while he was distracted you saw Moe peek at Larry's cards . . .

so you told Larry and Larry got cross and kicked
Moe off his chair . . .

and Moe landed on Pat, who
was reading to Bill and Phil . . .

and Pat's head jerked up,
flipping Bill and Phil into the air . . .

and Bill landed on the bench and knocked the
goldfish bowl . : .

which fell onto Fluffy's head . . .

making her look like an alien,
which scared Loompy and Laika . . .

and they barked so loudly they frightened Pink and
Mr. Hee-Haw . . .

so they stampeded . . .

and crashed head-on into
one another and then . . .

fell into the rabbits' wooden block tower . . .

which made the blocks go all over the floor . . .
period . . . the end."

Curly finishes his story and Jill laughs and shakes
her head. "Oh, you silly things!" she giggles. "I think
the *real* problem here is that it's dinner time and
you're all hungry, am I right?"

141

At the mention of the word "dinner," the animals get very excited. So does Terry. "What are we having?" he says.

"Well, it depends on what sort of animal you are," says Jill.

fluffy

YAY!

"The cats eat fish, the dogs eat bones, the donkey eats straw, the camel eats leaves, the horses eat hay, the rabbits eat carrots, the cow eats grass, the guinea pigs eat lettuce, the goldfish eat fish food and Manny, well, he eats everything—but, then, he *is* a goat."

"I'm a *human*," says Terry, "and I like to eat *marshmallows*."

"Me too," I say. "In fact, I'm on a marshmallow-only diet."

"I'm sorry," says Jill, "but we don't have any marshmallows. They're not good for the animals" teeth. But feel free to help yourself to any of our other food."

I look at Terry.

He looks at me.

We may not be able to understand animals like Jill can, but we can understand each other and what we're both thinking is *I don't like any of those foods, especially not grass!*

Mind you, in the end it doesn't really matter because once Jill bangs the dinner gong we can't even get near the table. The food is gone in about 30 seconds flat.

After our NO-dinner, we all play a game of pin-the-tail-on-Mr.-Hee-Haw . . .

which is kind of fun until Terry accidentally pins the tail on Mr. Hee-Haw's nose and Mr. Hee-Haw gets mad and bites Terry on the hand.

Luckily Jill has the rabbits well trained in first
aid—especially in how to treat donkey bites!
(I guess they must get a lot of practice around here.)

After Jill has read us—and all the animals—a
bedtime story, Terry and I say goodnight and go to
bed.

"Oh well," sighs Terry as we turn of the light.
"I'm a little bit hungry and my hand is sore, but at
least the bed is nice and big."

And it is, too, but then the door opens and the animals all pile into the bed with us.

"Hey, get out of here!" says Terry. "Go and sleep in your own bed!"

But the animals take no notice of him.

"I think this *is* their bed," I say. "That's what Jill was telling us earlier, but I couldn't hear her properly."

I don't know if you've ever tried to sleep in a bed full of animals, but I sure wouldn't recommend it.

The horses have galloping dreams,

the rabbits play hide-and-seek in the blankets,

the dogs sleep-bark,

and the goldfish play punk rock all night long.
(I don't know how, but their bowl ends up in the
bed with us as well.)

Things don't get any easier in the morning, either.
There's only *one* toilet,

one shower,

Soap

and *one* bowl of porridge.
(Sure, it's a *big* bowl, but it's animal-flavored—YUCK!)

"You know," says Terry, "I like Jill's house, but there's no place quite like home."

"You're right about that," I say. "I really miss the treehouse."

"So do I," says Terry. "I wish I'd never invented that stupid Once-upon-a-time machine!"

"Yeah, me too," I say. "If only you were as good at *un*-inventing things as you are at *in*venting them."

"Oh, you mean like Professor Stupido?" says Terry.

"*Who?*" I say.

"Professor Stupido, the famous un-inventor," says Terry.

"Ha, ha," I say. "Very funny."

"I'm not trying to be funny," he says. "There really *is* an un-inventor called Professor Stupido."

"But that's crazy," I say. "You can't *un*-invent things!"

"Oh yeah?" says Terry. "Well what about *frogpotamuses*?"

"Frogpotamuses?" I say. "There's no such thing."

"Not any more there's not," says Terry, "thanks to Professor Stupido! He *un*-invented them all. Every last one!"

He hands me a comic and says, "Here. Read this. It will explain everything!"

160

CHAPTER 8

PROFESSOR STUPIDO'S STORY

PROFESSOR STUPIDO, THE WORLD-FAMOUS UN-
INVENTOR, FIRST DISCOVERED HIS POWERS OF
UN-INVENTION AS A YOUNG BOY WHEN HIS WINDUP
TOY ROBOT REFUSED TO PLAY WITH HIM ONE DAY.

IN A RAGE, HE GRABBED A HAMMER,
RAISED IT HIGH ABOVE HIS HEAD AND
WITH ONE MIGHTY BLOW UN-INVENTED
HIS TOY ROBOT FOREVER!

NOT LONG AFTER UN-INVENTING
HIS TOY ROBOT, HE DISCOVERED
HE COULD ALSO UN-INVENT
BORING BOOKS.

Your plot is boring
And your characters dire.
I hereby un-invent you
Via the fire!

FLING!

AS PROFESSOR STUPIDO GREW OLDER, HE
BECAME CAPABLE OF EVER MORE DAZZLING
FEATS OF UN-INVENTION.

ONE DAY, WHILE OUT WALKING IN THE PARK, HE
SAW A HOT ICE-CREAM SELLER AND THOUGHT A
HOT ICE CREAM WOULD BE JUST THE THING TO
WARM HIM UP.

UNFORTUNATELY, THE HOT ICE CREAM WAS SO HOT THAT IT BURNED THE PROFESSOR'S TONGUE AND, IN A FIT OF RAGE, HE UN-INVENTED HOT ICE CREAM ON THE SPOT.

You burnt my tongue
And made me scream.
I un-invent you,
Hot ice cream!

WHILE THE PROFESSOR WAS HAPPY WITH HIS LATEST UN-INVENTION, HOWEVER, MANY HOT ICE CREAM LOVERS WERE NOT.

My Ice cream is freezing cold! I hate you PROFESSOR STUPIDO!

NOT LONG AFTER UN-INVENTING HOT ICE CREAM,
PROFESSOR STUPIDO'S INCREASINGLY AMAZING
POWERS OF UN-INVENTION WERE PUT TO THE
TEST WHEN HE WAS BUZZED BY A GANG OF
FLYING-BEETROOT RIDERS.

"BLAST AND CONFOUND THESE FLYING BEETROOTS," SAID PROFESSOR STUPIDO. "I'VE A GOOD MIND TO UN-INVENT THEM ONCE AND FOR ALL!"

"YOU CAN'T UN-INVENT FLYING BEETROOTS, OLD MAN!" SAID ONE OF THE BEETROOT RIDERS. "FLYING BEETROOTS ARE HERE TO STAY!"

"OH YEAH?" SAID PROFESSOR STUPIDO. "WE'LL SEE ABOUT THAT!"

Stupid flying beetroots
Whizzing through the air.
I hereby un-invent
Flying beetroots everywhere!

SUDDENLY THERE WAS NO SUCH THING
AS FLYING BEETROOTS ANY MORE AND THE
SURPRISED EX-FLYING-BEETROOT RIDERS
FELL FROM THE SKY AND CRASHED
TO THE GROUND.

PROFESSOR STUPIDO HAD SUCCESSFULLY UN-
INVENTED FLYING BEETROOTS, BUT, UNFORTUNATELY,
THE WORLD WAS NOW FULL OF BRUISED AND ANGRY
EX-FLYING-BEETROOT RIDERS.

ONE AFTERNOON,
PROFESSOR STUPIDO
WAS OUT TAKING HIS
DAILY STROLL, THINKING
OF NEW THINGS TO
UN-INVENT...

WHEN A 10-TON
FROGPOTAMUS
JUMPED OUT OF A
TREE...

AND
ATTACHED
ITSELF TO
HIS HEAD!

"BLAST AND CONFOUND THESE STUPID FROGPOTAMUSES ALWAYS JUMPING OUT OF TREES AND ATTACHING THEMSELVES TO MY HEAD!" YELLED PROFESSOR STUPIDO. "I'M GOING TO UN-INVENT THE LOT OF THEM!"

AND SO HE DID.

NOT EVERYBODY, HOWEVER, WAS HAPPY WITH THE PROFESSOR'S LATEST UN-INVENTION . . . ESPECIALLY NOT THE ROYAL SOCIETY OF FROGPOTAMUS SPOTTERS.

"OH NO, WHAT HAVE YOU DONE?" YELLED THE PRESIDENT OF THE ROYAL SOCIETY OF FROGPOTAMUS SPOTTERS.

"I'VE UN-INVENTED FROGPOTAMUSES, THAT'S WHAT!" SAID PROFESSOR STUPIDO. "THANKS TO ME, NOBODY WILL HAVE THEIR HEAD SWALLOWED BY A FROGPOTAMUS EVER AGAIN!"

"BUT YOU'VE MADE THEM EXTINCT!" SAID THE PRESIDENT. "WHAT WILL WE FROGPOTAMUS SPOTTERS SPOT NOW?!"

UNFORTUNATELY FOR PROFESSOR STUPIDO, IT
WASN'T ONLY FROGPOTAMUS SPOTTERS, FLYING-
BEETROOT RIDERS AND HOT ICE CREAM FANS WHO
FAILED TO APPRECIATE HIS GENIUS. SOON THE
WHOLE WORLD WAS UNITED AGAINST HIM AND HIS
UN-INVENTIONS.

FINALLY THE PEOPLE OF EARTH HAD A BIG MEETING
AND VOTED TO UN-INVENT PROFESSOR STUPIDO.
THEY PICKED HIM UP . . .

TIED HIM TO A ROCKET...

AND BLASTED HIM TO THE DARK SIDE OF THE MOON, WHERE HE WOULDN'T BE ABLE TO ANNOY THEM WITH HIS STUPID UN-INVENTIONS EVER AGAIN.

THE END

CHAPTER 9

THE DARK SIDE OF THE MOON

"See?" says Terry. "What did I tell you? There *is* such a thing as an un-inventor. And Professor Stupido is the best un-inventor in the world."

177

"Yes," I say, "I can see that, but the only problem is he's not *in* the world—he's on the dark side of the moon. How would we even get in touch with him?"

"Easy!" says Terry. "We get a rocket, fly to the moon, find him and bring him back. What could be easier—or more simple—than that?"

"Um, well, nothing," I say, "except for the fact that we don't *have* a rocket."

"No, not at the moment," says Terry, "but I could draw one."

"How are you going to do that?" I say. "Your drawing hand is all bandaged up, remember?"

"Oh yeah," says Terry. "I forgot."

"I guess *I* could try," I say.

"I don't think that's such a good idea, Andy," says Terry. "You can't draw, remember?"

"Not as well as you, no, but I think I could draw a rocket, I mean, how hard could it be to draw a rectangle with a triangle on the top? Watch this!"

I pick up a pen and draw a rocket. But it's not quite as easy as I thought.

by Andy

"No offense, Andy," says Terry, "but that's pretty much the worst drawing of a rocket I've ever seen."

"There's something wrong with the pen!" I say.

"The pen is fine," says Terry. "I think it's you that's the problem. But I've got an idea. How about I do a dot-to-dot rocket? Then all you have to do is join the dots."

"I don't know," I say. "I'm not very good at dot-to-dot pictures. They're really hard."

"Don't worry," says Terry. "I'll make it really easy for you."

Terry takes the pen with his good hand and starts dotting the air in front of us.

"There's your dots, Andy," he says when he's finished. "Now all you have to do is join them up. Good luck!"

He hands me the pen.
   I start connecting the dots.

"It doesn't look much like a rocket to me," I say, as I join the last dot.

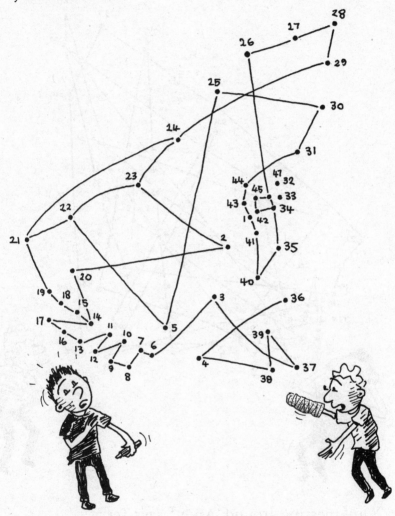

"That's because you didn't do it right," says Terry. "Erase it and try again."

I try again but this time it's even worse.

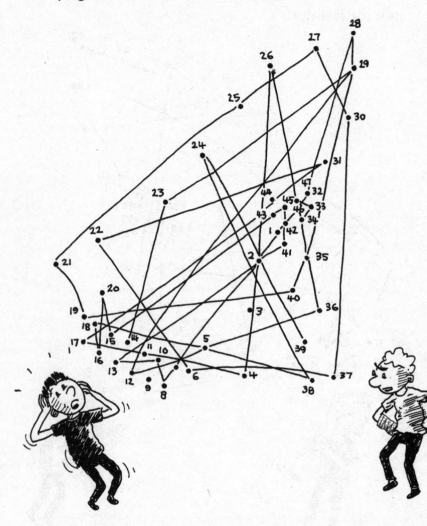

"Quit messing around, Andy," says Terry.

"I'm not!" I say, erasing the lines. "Let me have one more go."

This time I try curvy lines, but it still doesn't look much like a rocket.

"That's hopeless!" says Terry. "Why don't you just follow the numbers?"

"Um . . ." I say. "You know how I can't really draw?"

"Yes."

"Well, I can't really count, either."

"You can't count?!" says Terry.

"Well, I can a little bit," I say, "just not in the right order. I had a very bad teacher."

"Wow," says Terry. "I see what you mean. How about I help you count? I'll say the numbers and all you have to do is draw the lines—*straight* lines—between the dots."

"I don't know," I say. "That sounds kind of complicated."

"You can do it, Andy," says Terry. "I'll start you off. One."

"One," I say, putting the tip of the pencil on the dot next to the number 1.

"Two," says Terry.

"Two," I say, drawing a line from dot number 1 to dot number 2.

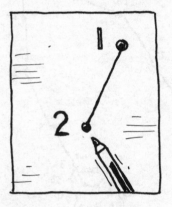

"Three," says Terry.

"Three," I say, drawing a line from dot number 2 to dot number 3.

"That's it, Andy," says Terry. "You're really getting the hang of it. Let's keep going. Four . . ."

Forty-seven dots later, we have a surprisingly well-drawn dot-to-dot rocket.

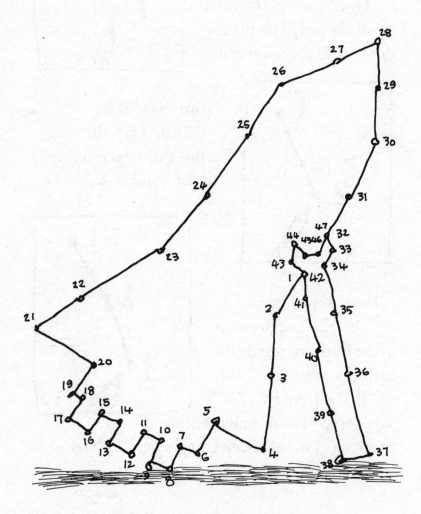

"Wow! I DID IT!" I say. "I joined the dots! I'm a GENIUS!"

"I *knew* you could do it!" says Terry. "Now all we need is some windows and we're good to go."

I draw a couple of circles on the rocket. "How's that?" I say.

"They'll do nicely," says Terry. "Start the countdown, Andy."

191

THE DAY OUR ROCKET WENT COMPLETELY OUT OF CONTROL ALL OVER THE UNIVERSE AND THEN CRASH-LANDED ON THE MOON

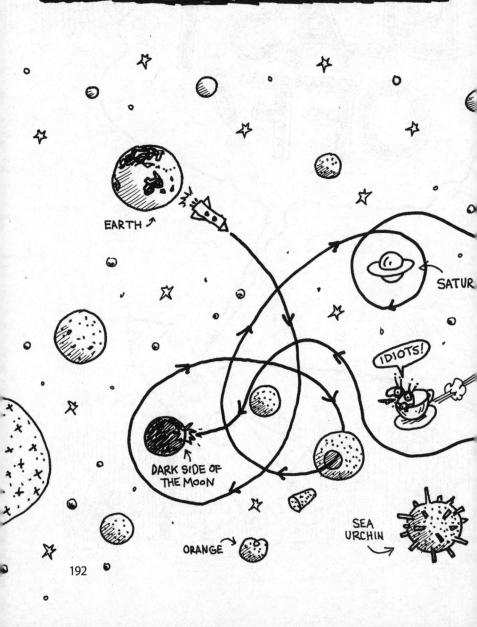

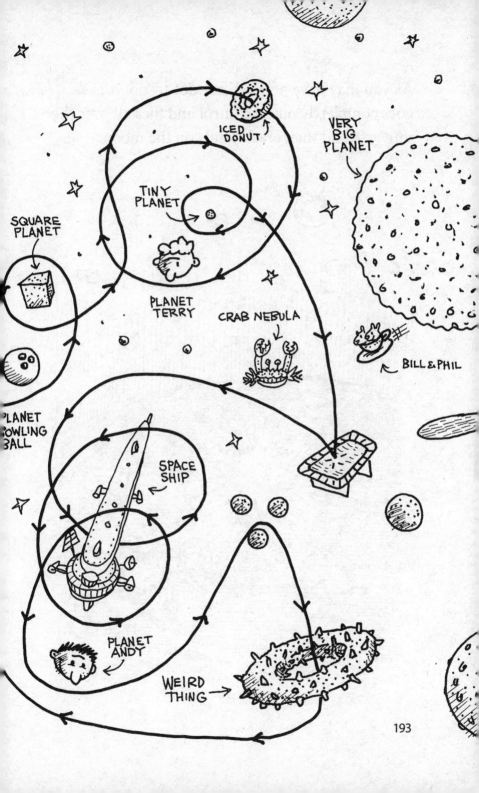

ICED DONUT

VERY BIG PLANET

TINY PLANET

SQUARE PLANET

PLANET TERRY

CRAB NEBULA

BILL & PHIL

PLANET BOWLING BALL

SPACE SHIP

PLANET ANDY

WEIRD THING

193

As you may have noticed, our dot-to-dot rocket goes completely out of control and flies all over the universe and then crash-lands on the moon.

"I wonder which side of the moon we are on?" says Terry.

"Well," I say, "judging by the position of the stars, and the relative lack of light, I'd say we're on the dark side."

"Wow," says Terry, "you may not be very good at drawing or counting but you sure know your way around the universe, Andy!"

"Not really," I say, "but I'm quite good at reading and that sign over there says 'THE DARK SIDE OF THE MOON'."

"Brilliant!" says Terry. "And isn't that Professor Stupido heading this way?"

"I think you're right," I say. "But he doesn't look too happy to see us."

"WHO ARE YOU?" yells Professor Stupido. "And what are these numbers and dots doing all over my nice clean moon?"

"Sorry about that," I say. "I'm Andy and this is my friend Terry and the numbers and dots are the remains of our dot-to-dot rocket. We had a bit of a rough landing. But don't worry, we'll clean it all up."

"Well, see that you do!" says Professor Stupido. "I don't like mess—or uninvited visitors. In fact, I've got a good mind to un-invent the pair of you!"

"No, wait," says Terry, "please don't!"

"Give me one good reason why I shouldn't," says Professor Stupido.

"Because we're your biggest fans!" says Terry.

"You are?" he says. "I thought everybody on Earth hated me."

"Not us!" says Terry. "We think you're the greatest un-inventor who ever lived."

"Oh, I don't know about that," says Professor Stupido.

"Yes you are!" says Terry. "You're a *genius*!"

"Well, yes, I suppose you're right," says the professor. "I mean any bozo can invent things … but it takes real skill to *un-invent* them."

"Exactly!" says Terry. "And that's why we're here. We need to ask you a *huge* favor."

"And what might that be?" says Professor Stupido.

Terry takes a deep breath. "Can you come to our treehouse and un-invent a machine for us?"

"Not on your life," says Professor Stupido. "I'm not going back to Earth. Those ignorant fools down there don't appreciate my genius. They strapped me to a giant firework and sent me on a one-way ride to the dark side of the moon."

"Yes, we know," says Terry, "but this is different because we're *asking* you to un-invent something. *Please!* You're the only one who can help us."

"I don't know ..." says Professor Stupido.

"Please?" I say.

"Pretty please?" says Terry.

"Pretty please with sugar on top?" I add.

"Pretty please with sugar and a *marshmallow* on top?" says Terry.

"Hmmm," says Professor Stupido, "marshmallows you say?"

"Yes!" says Terry. "We've got a machine that follows you around and fires marshmallows into your mouth whenever you're hungry!"

"Well, I can see why you would want me to un-invent a machine like that," says Professor Stupido. "It sounds *very* annoying."

"No, not *that* machine," I say. "We *like* that machine. It's the Once-upon-a-time machine we want you to un-invent."

"A *time* machine?" says Professor Stupido. "I've always wanted to *un*-invent one of those."

"No," says Terry. "It's a *Once-upon-a-time* machine. I invented it to write and draw books, but it's taken over and won't let us back into our treehouse because it thinks it writes better books than we do."

"That's outrageous," says Professor Stupido. "Machines need to know their place. It would give me great pleasure to un-invent an upstart machine like that."

"So you'll do it?" says Terry.

"Yes, I will!" says Professor Stupido. "When can we leave?"

"Just as soon as we get our rocket back together," I say.

Terry and I collect all the numbers and dots and redraw our rocket as fast as we can before Professor Stupido changes his mind.

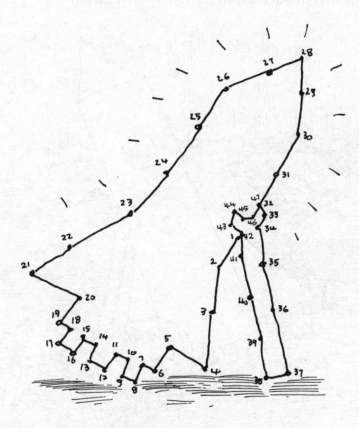

It's not long before we have a brand-new rocket ready to take us all back to Earth.

"Hmmm, dot-to-dot rocket, eh?" says Professor Stupido, walking all around it. "What an ingenious combination of dots, numbers and pen lines. It would be both a great challenge and an honor to un-invent such an imaginative invention!"

"NO!" I yell. "We need it to get back to Earth!"

"Relax," chuckles Professor Stupido as we all climb into the rocket. "I was only joking. I think you'll find that as well as being the world's greatest un-inventor, I also have the world's greatest sense of humor!"

"Okay, Andy," says Terry. "Start the countdown!"
I concentrate as hard as I can and begin . . .

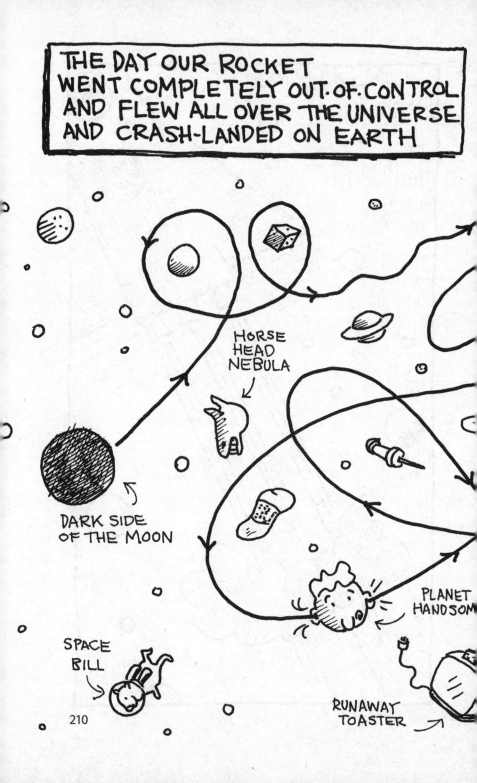

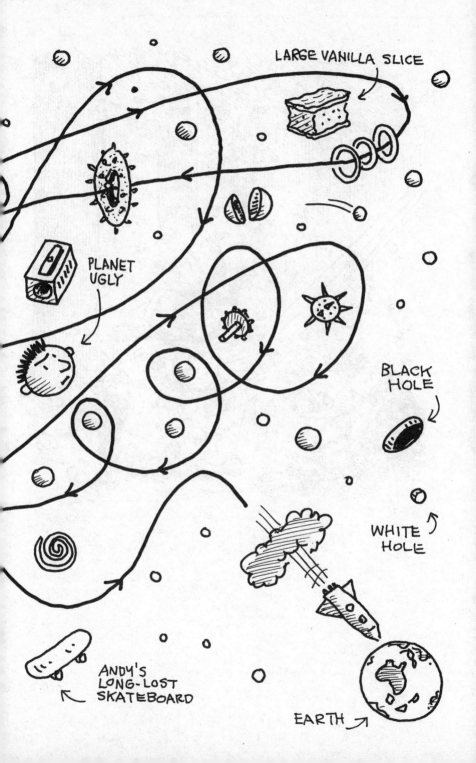

LARGE VANILLA SLICE

PLANET UGLY

BLACK HOLE

WHITE HOLE

ANDY'S LONG-LOST SKATEBOARD

EARTH

CHAPTER 10

BLOOF! BLOORT! BLAP!

"Ouch, my aching head!" says Professor Stupido. "Where are we?"

"Well," I say, "judging by the grass, the shade and all the trees, I'd say we're in some sort of forest."

"I think you're right, Andy," says Terry, "because, look, over there is a sign saying 'SOME SORT OF FOREST'."

"Actually," I say, looking around, "that's one of *your* signs and this is *our* forest."

"Yes!" says Terry. "And there's our treehouse!"

"Uh-oh . . ." I say. "Watch out! Here come the hands!"

"What's happening?" says Professor Stupido.
"It's the machine we were telling you about,"
I say. "It slaps us away whenever we get too close
to the treehouse."

"I'll soon put a stop to that," says Professor Stupido.

217

"Yay!" says Terry. "Thanks, Professor! You're the best!"

"Don't mention it," says Professor Stupido. "Is there anything else you would like un-invented while I'm at it?"

"No, that won't be necessary," I say quickly, before he can un-invent anything we don't want un-invented. "I expect you'll be wanting to get back to the dark side of the moon now, so we'll just draw another rocket and get you on your way."

"Hold on," says the professor, "not so fast. What about those marshmallows I was promised?"

"Come inside," says Terry, "and have as many as you like! And we've also got a lemonade fountain, a chocolate waterfall and a 78-flavor ice-cream parlor!"

"It's not *hot* ice cream is it?" says the professor suspiciously. "I hate hot ice cream!"

"No, it's cold ice cream," says Terry. "That's the only sort we have on Earth now. You un-invented hot ice cream, remember?"

"Oh, so I did!" he chuckles. "I've un-invented so many things it's hard to keep track of them all!"

We let ourselves into the treehouse and as soon as we're inside the marshmallow machine senses how hungry we are and starts firing marshmallows at us.

Terry and I open our mouths and start swallowing as fast as we can. But Professor Stupido puts up his hands and yells, "Oh no, we're under attack again!"

"No, we're not," I try to explain through a mouthful of marshmallows. "The marshmallow machine is just doing what it's supposed to."

But I don't think Professor Stupido understands me because he points at the machine and says:

Suddenly, the marshmallow machine is gone.

"You idiot!" yells Terry. "You un-invented our marshmallow machine! What are we going to eat now?"

Uh-oh. I haven't known Professor Stupido for very long but I'm guessing he's not the sort of person you should call an idiot.

"Did I hear correctly, boy?" says the professor, glaring at Terry. "Did you just call me an idiot?"

Terry looks terrified.

"Uh, er, um . . ." he stammers.

"Well?" says the professor. "I'm waiting!"

"NO!" says Terry, thinking faster than I've ever seen him think before. "I said, 'Thanks for getting *rid of it*!'"

Professor Stupido beams at Terry. "Oh, don't mention it," he says. "Nothing gives me more pleasure than to un-invent annoying and dangerous things. And speaking of dangerous, is that a tank of man-eating sharks I see?"

"Y-yes," I say nervously, "but they're not dangerous, they only eat fish."

"They *did* eat Captain Woodenhead, though," says Terry.

"So they *are* man-eaters!" says the professor. "I knew it! I'll have them un-invented in a jiffy."

"Please don't un-invent them," I say. "Man-eating sharks are cool!"

"They're not cool, they're cruel!" says the professor. "And that's exactly why I'm going to un-invent them. Stand back!"

Their teeth are big and pointy
And they chew up men for fun.
I hereby un-invent all sharks,
Yes, each and every one!

BLAP!

I stare at the empty shark tank.

I think Professor Stupido may have become a bigger threat to the treehouse than the Once-upon-a-time machine.

We have to get rid of him—and fast!

But before I can say—or do—anything . . .

a bowling ball falls through the air . . .

narrowly misses Professor Stupido's head . . .

and crashes down onto the floor beside him.

"Oh my goodness!" says Professor Stupido. "Is there a bowling alley up there?"

"Yeah," says Terry. "Our treehouse has got *everything*!"

"Not any more it hasn't," says Professor Stupido.

I won't waste time or pause
Or delay or dilly-dally.
I'll un-invent at once
That annoying bowling alley.

"Oh no!" I say. "There goes our bowling alley!"

"Yes," says Terry, "but look on the bright side— at least he didn't un- invent the penguins."

"Penguins?" says Professor Stupido. "Did you say *penguins*? Can't stand them! They're even worse than frogpotamuses! I'll un-invent them right away!"

The penguin is a silly bird
With useless little wings.
I hereby un-invent them all,
Those stupid, flightless things.

BLOORT!

Professor Stupido has barely finished un-inventing penguins when the doorbell rings.

"What's that annoying ringing noise?" he says.

"It's just the doorbell," I say quickly. "But please don't un-invent it or we won't know when someone's at the door."

"All right," sighs the professor. "I won't un-invent your precious doorbell."

"Hi, Andy! Hi, Terry!" calls a familiar voice. "Mail!"

"Who's that?" says Professor Stupido.

"It's Bill," says Terry. "Bill the postman!"

"Any mail for me?" says the professor.

"I'll just check," says Bill. "What's your name?"

"Professor Stupido," he says.

"I'm afraid not," says Bill.

"Blast it all!" says the professor. "I *hate* not getting mail. Consider yourself—and all your kind—un-invented, Bill the postman."

I hereby un-invent
Postal workers everywhere.
How will people get their mail?
I tell you, I don't care!

BLAP!

Poor Bill!

Terry and I look at each other but don't dare say a thing.

Professor Stupido yawns. "All this un-inventing has made me tired," he says. "I think I'll have a little rest."

"Phew!" I whisper to Terry. "At least he won't be able to un-invent anything while he's asleep."

Professor Stupido has only been gone for a few minutes when the loudest guitar solo you ever heard fills the treehouse.

There's only one guitar player on Earth who can play that loudly. Well, maybe two. And I'm pretty sure Professor Stupido is not going to like either of them.

Professor Stupido climbs back down the ladder.
"I can't sleep," he shouts over the music. "What is
that awful racket?"

"That's not an awful racket," says Terry. "That's Jimi
Handrix and Superfinger. They're playing at the
opera house."

"Not any more they're not!" says Professor
Stupido.

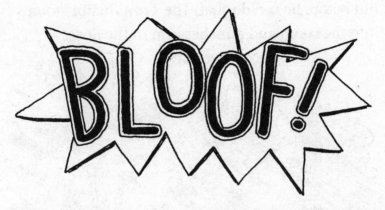

"Oh no," says Terry. "You un-invented *Jimi Handrix*!"

"And Superfinger!" I say. "What will all the people with problems requiring finger-based solutions do now?"

"I can fix that," says the professor. "I'll just un-invent problems requiring finger-based solutions."

But before he can do that, The Trunkinator stomps into the room and punches him in the nose.

"What was that for?" says the professor, looking up at The Trunkinator.

"I think he's upset about you un-inventing Jimi Handrix," says Terry.

"Yeah. He's a big fan," I say. "Possibly the biggest."

The professor tries to get up but The Trunkinator smashes him back down and starts flattening him like a pancake.

"Right, that's it, pal!" shouts the professor. "You're un-invented!"

BLOOF!

I hereby un-invent Your boxing Trunkinator— I guess it's fair to say that I'm a Trunkinator-Hater!

Suddenly the tree starts to shake.

"What's that?" I say. "What's happening now?"

"It sounds like The Trunkinator stomping around," says Terry.

"But The Trunkinator just got un-invented," I say.

"Then it must be the volcano," says Terry. "I think it's erupting!"

"But when you put it in you promised me it was the non-erupting kind!" I say.

"I know," says Terry. "But it looks like I was wrong. Anyone can make a little mistake."

"This is not a 'little mistake'!" I yell. "It's a HUGE DISASTER!"

"No problem," says the professor. "I'll just un-invent volcanoes!"

"But I *love* volcanoes!" says Terry.

"So you'd rather be covered in red-hot lava?" says the professor incredulously.

"Um, let me think," says Terry.

"It's not something you need to think about,
Terry!" I say. I turn to the professor. "Un-invent
volcanoes . . . quick!"

"Consider it done," says the professor.

I do not like volcanoes
That smoke and spit and spew.
I interrupt your eruption
By un-inventing you!

"Oh no," says Terry. "How are we going to toast our marshmallows now?"

"Don't worry about it," I say. "There's no such thing as marshmallows any more, remember? Professor Stupido un-invented them."

"Oh yeah," says Terry sadly. "I remember."

That's when we hear the unmistakable sound of Professor Stupido un-inventing something else.

"Uh-oh," says Terry. "What
has he un-invented now?"
"I don't know," I say.

"But I've got a terrible feeling he's not going to be
happy until he has un-invented EVERYTHING!"

CHAPTER 11

BLAM! BLOOT! BLING!

"STOP!" I yell.
But Professor Stupido doesn't stop.
He keeps right on un-inventing . . .

and un-inventing . . .

and un-inventing . . .

and un-inventing . . .

until all that is left of our treehouse is the tree.

"Our *treehouse!*" says Terry. "Our *39-story treehouse!* It's gone! All gone! You've un-invented the whole thing! Now it's nothing but a 39-story-*less* tree!"

"Hmm," says Professor Stupido, stroking his chin. "Good point. I'll un-invent that for you as well . . ."

This tree serves no purpose,
As far as I can see.
There ... it's un-invented
And it's all thanks to me!

BLING!

"Our tree!" I say. "You un-invented our tree!"

"I think you'll find that one tree is very much like another," says Professor Stupido, "and there's plenty more trees in the forest. Which makes me think that I may as well un-invent the rest of them while I'm at it."

What use to us are forests?
They're just a bunch of trees.
I'll un-invent the lot of them—
The trunks, the twigs, the leaves!

BLAM!

"But what about all the birds and animals?" says Terry. "Where will they live now?"

"No need to worry about that," says Professor Stupido. "I'll just un-invent them."

I'll un-invent the birds
And all the earthly creatures,
Especially the snakes
And those awful, sucky leeches!

BLOOT!

"Ah, that's better," says Professor Stupido. "And now that I've rid the world of all those pesky animals, I may as well finish the job and un-invent humans too."

Terry and I gasp.

"Don't worry," chuckles Professor Stupido. "I'll un-invent everybody except you. After all, you're the only ones who understand and appreciate my genius."

"Oh no!" I say. "I think you've gone too far this time!"

"On the contrary," says Professor Stupido calmly. "I don't think I've gone nearly far enough. Imagine, if you will, a world in which there's not only no people but there's also *no world!*"

"I can't imagine *a world with no world,*" says Terry. "It doesn't make any sense!"

"It makes *perfect* sense to me," says Professor Stupido. "In fact, the very idea of it makes me want to sing!"

Imagine a world
That has been un-invented.
Think of all the problems
That will now be prevented!

No boxing elephants
To punch your nose.
No crabs at the beach
To pinch your toes.

No polluting pollution,
No smoking smokestacks,
No overcrowded
Confusing bike racks.

No spots or pimples
Or itchy rashes.
No tripping or falling
Or nasty crashes.

No waste, no garbage,
No junk and no litter,
No texting, no Facebook,
No spam and no Twitter.

No noise or fuss,
No bother or mess,
No need to worry
Or fret or stress.

No more noisy
Sporting events,
No more rained-out
Vacations in tents.

No more warnings
About global-warming.
No more boring
Boy bands forming.

No more fights
Or bites or bruises.
No more winners,
No more losers.

Nothing to lose,
Nothing to gain.
No more struggling
And no more pain.

How clean, how pure
And perfectly silent.
How wonderfully peaceful
And not at all violent.

Nobody could possibly
Be discontented
In a world that I
Have un-invented!

We are floating in the space where the world used to be.

"Oh well," says Terry. "Our world might be gone but let's look on the bright side."

"What bright side?!" I say.

"Well at least we've still got the moon, the sun and all the planets."

"Thanks for reminding me," says Professor Stupido. "I'll take care of them right away!"

There's a blinding flash and then no more solar system.

"Oh, well, no use crying over un-invented solar systems," says Terry. "At least he didn't un-invent the whole universe."

"What a good idea!" says Professor Stupido. "Thank you so much, Terry! I'll get right on to it."

"You and your big mouth, Terry!" I say.

"Relax," he says. "As if he could even *do* that!"

Professor Stupido takes a deep breath.

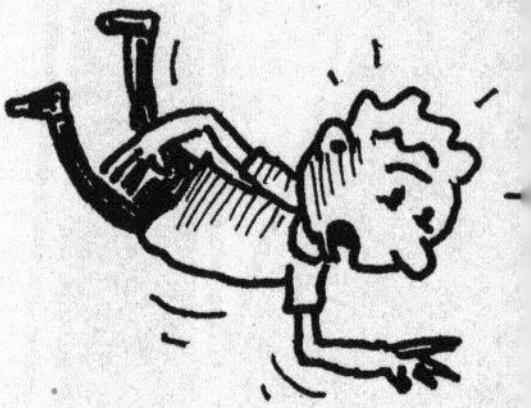

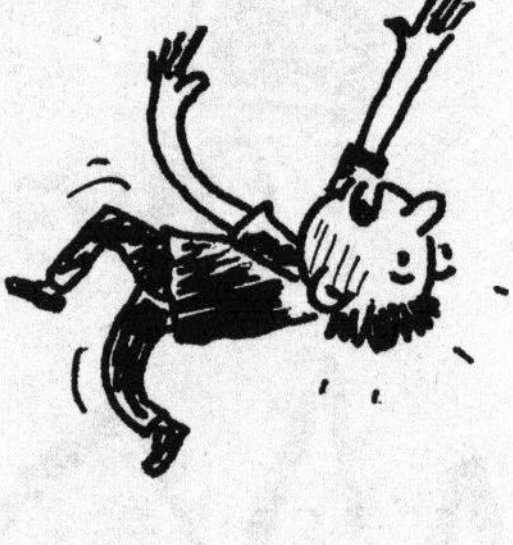

"I've done it!" says Professor Stupido. "I've un-invented the entire universe! Nobody has ever un-invented this much stuff before. I'm definitely without doubt the greatest un-inventor who ever lived!"

"What are we going to do?" I whisper to Terry. "It's only a matter of time before he un-invents *us* as well!"

"I know," says Terry. "I wish he would un-invent *himself*!"

"That's it!" I say.

"What?"

"We'll challenge him to un-invent himself," I say. "What do you think?"

"It's definitely worth a try!" says Terry. "If anyone could do it, he could."

"Hey, Professor!" I say. "We just thought of something you *can't* un-invent."

"Ridiculous!" says the professor. "There is *nothing* I can't un-invent!"

"What about *yourself*?" says Terry. "I bet you can't un-invent *that*!"

"Of course I can un-invent myself," says Professor Stupido, "but why would I want to deprive us all of the greatest un-inventor who ever lived?"

"Oh, no reason," I say, "except perhaps to prove beyond all doubt that you actually *could* un-invent yourself."

"But we all *know* I could," says the professor. "I mean, I un-invented the entire universe—to un-invent myself would be child's play in comparison!"

"Do you know what I think?" says Terry. "I think you're chicken!"

"I am NOT chicken!"

"Yes you are!"

"No I'm not!"

"Yes you are!"

"No I'm not!"

"Yes you are!"

"No I'm not!"

"Yes you are!"

"No I'm not!"

"Yes you are!"

"No I'm not!"

"Yes you are!"

"No I'm not!"

"Yes you are!"

"No I'm *NOT*," says Professor Stupido, "and I'll prove it, once and for all!"

"We did it!" I say. "We tricked Professor Stupido into un-inventing himself!"

"Well, what are we waiting for?" says Terry. "Let's get back to the treehouse!"

"There's just one little problem," I say. "There is no treehouse ... no treehouse, no tree, no *anything*. He un-invented *everything*. *Every single thing.*"

"No problem," says Terry. "Stand clear!"

"Why?" I say. "What are you going to do?"

"I'm going to draw it all back again," says Terry.

CHAPTER 12

THE AMAZING
SPOONCIL!

"But you can't redraw a whole universe!" I say.
"I mean, I *know* you're a good drawer—and I admit
that you're *much* better than me—but … a whole
universe? *Really?!*"

"Sure!" says Terry. "Universes aren't quite as complicated as you might think. You just start with a big bang, a bit of space, a few trillion suns, a couple of billion planets, a bunch of moons, a black hole or two, and take it from there."

"But what about your sore hand?" I say.

"It's not sore any more!" says Terry. "When Professor Stupido un-invented bites and bruises it got better *instantly*!"

"Well, that's great," I say, "but he also un-invented pens and pencils."

"That doesn't matter," says Terry. "I've got a *spooncil*!"

"What's a spooncil?"

"It's half spoon and half pencil!" says Terry. "I made it myself. Check out the ad!"

"Wow, that's brilliant!" I say. "But how come you've still got it? Didn't Professor Stupido un-invent spooncils as well?"

"It's the only one of its kind," says Terry, "which is maybe why he couldn't un-invent it—he didn't know it existed. Well, that and the fact that I keep it hidden up my nose."

"You keep it hidden up your nose?" I say. "*Why?*"

"For emergencies, of course," says Terry, "just like this one. The only problem is that it's quite far up. Can you help me get it out?"

"No way!" I say. "I'm not putting my finger up your nose!"

"But the fate of the whole entire universe depends on it!"

"I DON'T CARE!" I say. "I'm *still* not putting my finger up your nose!"

"Never mind," says Terry. "I think I feel a sneeze coming on."

"Excellent!"

Terry tilts his head back. "Ah … ah … ah …"

I cover my face. Terry's sneezes can be pretty messy.

"Nah . . . sorry," says Terry. "False alarm."

"That's a pity," I say.

"No, wait," says Terry, "here it comes again."

"Thank goodness!" I say.

"Ah … ah … ah …"

"Nah," says Terry. "Another false alarm."

"Oh well," I say. "I guess we're just going to have to float around in nothingness forever."

"Andy?" says Terry.

"What?" I say. "Is your sneeze coming back?"

"No, I just wanted to say that if I have to float around in nothingness for the rest of my life there's no one I'd rather do it with than . . . AH-CHOO!"

"Oh gross, Terry!" I say. "You sneezed right in my face! That's the grossest thing you've ever done!"

"I don't think so," says Terry. "I'd say it's more like the third-grossest."

I think for a moment. "Yeah," I say, "you're probably right."

291

"Sorry about that, Andy," says Terry, "but at least I got my spooncil out!"

"Before you start redrawing the universe," I say, "do you think you could possibly draw me a handkerchief?"

"Sure, there you go," says Terry. "Now, if you'll excuse me, I'd better get started …"

As I watch, Terry draws stars, planets and moons . . .

UFOs, black holes, comets, meteorites, supernovas, red dwarfs, terrifying aliens and hideous monsters that I thought only existed in science fiction comics.

"Yikes!" I say.

"Calm down, Andy," says Terry, "it's just a razor-toothed, Venusian blood-sucking worm-man!"

"I know," I say, "but do you really have to draw it?"

"Yes," he says, "I have to draw everything back exactly the way it was before!"

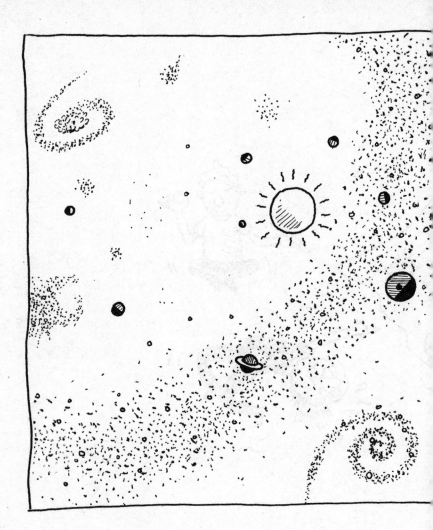

Terry draws the entire Milky Way Galaxy,
including the sun and the moon and all the planets:
Mars, Mercury, Venus, Saturn, Jupiter, Neptune,
Uranus and the most important one of all—Earth!

"YAY! Earth!" I say. "Can we go there right now?"

"Not so fast, Andy," says Terry. "I have to draw all the stuff on it first."

"Well, hurry up!" I say. "I never thought I'd say this, but I'm really missing gravity . . . plus I also need to go to the bathroom."

Terry draws everything on the Earth's surface,
including the oceans, the mountains, the deserts,
the forests, the savannas and the swamps.

He draws all the roads and buildings, including houses, hospitals, sporting stadiums, schools, shops and roadside stalls.

"Hey, that's pretty good," I say. "Can I do some?"

"Thanks for the offer, Andy," says Terry, "but it's probably better if you let me do it. In fact, promise me that you won't draw *anything*."

"Okay," I say, "I promise."

Terry starts drawing all the animals on Earth.

"Don't bother drawing all the rabbits," I say.
"Two will be enough."

"Why?" says Terry.

"Don't worry," I say. "Just keep drawing. I'll tell you about the rabbits later."

It doesn't take long before Terry has got everything almost back to normal, including the forest, our tree and our treehouse—all 39 levels!

CHAPTER 13

THE LAST CHAPTER

Terry sighs. "There," he says, "that's it."

"I think you forgot something," I say.

"What?"

"Jill!" I say.

"Oops," says Terry. "One Jill coming right up!"

"How's that?" says Terry.
  "Too tall," I say.

Terry draws her again.
  "How about this?"
he says.
  "Too short."

"What about this?"
says Terry.
  "Just right!" I say.

Jill blushes.

Terry giggles.

I look around to see what's so funny. Terry has drawn love hearts just above my head.

"Terry!" I say. "Cut it out."

"Sorry, Andy," says Terry, removing them with his laser-eraser. "How's that?"

"Much better," I say.

"Okay," says Terry. "Well, if you two *lovebirds* will excuse me, I'd better go and finish coloring in all the fish in the sea."

He runs off laughing.

"What's going on?" says Jill. "All my animals disappeared . . . and then *I* disappeared!"

"Yeah, sorry about that," I say. "I'm afraid you and your animals got un-invented."

"*Un-invented?*" says Jill. "How?"

"Professor Stupido, the famous un-inventor, did it," I explain. "We asked him to un-invent our Once-upon-a-time machine but he ended up un-inventing the whole universe, including himself. Terry's only just finished drawing everything back again."

"What about Silky?" says Jill. "Is she all right?"

I look around but I can't see her anywhere.

"I think Terry might have forgotten about Silky," I say.

Jill's eyes fill with tears.

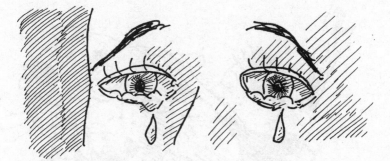

"Don't cry," I say quickly. "I'll fix it."

"How?" says Jill.

"I'll draw you a new Silky."

"I didn't think you could draw," she says.

"Not as well as Terry, no, but how hard could it be to draw a flying cat?" I say. "They're just a few circles, whiskers, wings and a tail."

I try to draw Silky as best as I can, but she doesn't come out quite right. In fact, she doesn't look like a flying cat at all. More like a mutant-lion kind of thing.

I'm trying to draw its ears on when it looks at me with its badly drawn eyes and starts growling.

"Andy!" cries Jill. "What have you drawn?!"

"To tell you the truth," I say, "I'm not quite sure. Can you talk to it and try to calm it down?"

"I can't talk to it," says Jill. "It doesn't have any ears!"

"We'd better call Terry, then," I say.

"HELP!" we both yell. "TERRY! HELP! COME QUICKLY!"

Terry comes running, his laser-eraser in his hand.

"Stand back," he says as he drops to one knee
and takes aim.

When he's finished, he turns to me and says,
"You promised you wouldn't draw *anything*."

"How do you know *I* drew it?" I say.

"Only *you* could draw something as badly drawn
as that," he says, shaking his head.

"Well I wouldn't have had to draw *anything* if
you'd remembered to draw Silky."

"I *did* draw Silky," he says, "*and* all her friends!
Look, here they are now!"

We look up.

The sky is filled with flying cats.

While Jill hugs Silky and all her other flying cats, my jet-chair appears and I fly up into the treehouse.

It's all just exactly as it was before. The tank full of man-eating sharks,

the bowling alley,

the opera house,

and even the Once-
upon-a-time
machine . . .

Hang on!!!

The Once-upon-a-time
machine???????????????
What's THAT doing
here???????????????????
"TERRY!" I yell.

Terry appears, closely followed by Jill.

"What's the matter?" he says.

"*That's* what's the matter!" I say, pointing at the machine. "Why did you redraw the *Once-upon-a-time machine* after we went to all that trouble to get rid of it?"

"I *didn't* redraw it!" he says.

"Then how come it's here?" I say.

Terry thinks for a moment. "It must have redrawn itself!" he says.

"Oh, great!" I say. "Then that means the last 142 pages have all been for nothing!"

"Well at least it's not switched on," says Jill, "otherwise it wouldn't have let us into the treehouse."

"You're right," says Terry, "and look—there's a manuscript in the print-out chute. It must have finished our book!"

"Let me see!" I say.

"Me, too!" says Jill.

We read the book ...

the greatest invention that Terry—or anyone else—has ever invented.

"That's terrible!" says Terry.

"I know," says Bill, "but that's not even the worst thing they do."

"What could they possibly do that is worse than stealing a child's birthday money?" I say.

"I'll tell you what," says Bill. "Sometimes they intercept the children's birthday party invitations as well!

Then they go around to the houses where the birthday parties are being held . . .

and steal the balloons right off the front gate!

"I've just thought of one more thing," I say. "Can we have an explosion?"

"No problem," says Terry, setting the arrow to EXPLOSION on the DISASTER dial.

EXPLOSION
EARTHQUAKE
LIGHTNING STRIKE
METEOR SHOWER
ALIEN INVASION
MR. BIG NOSE
SUPER NOVA BLAST

82

"I think we've almost got everything we need," says Terry. "Is there anything else you can think of?"
"Surprise me," I say.

FRUIT AND VEGETABLE-BASED TRANSPORT OPTIONS
CRUISING CARROT
FLYING BEETROOT
FLOATING PEACH
HIGH-SPEED WATERMELON
SINKING STRAWBERRY
ROCKET-PROPELLED EGGPLANT

"Okay," says Terry, giggling. "You're going to love this."

83

We fly up into the air, up over the forest and far, far away.

And then we start to fall down, slowly at first then faster and faster and faster . . .

322

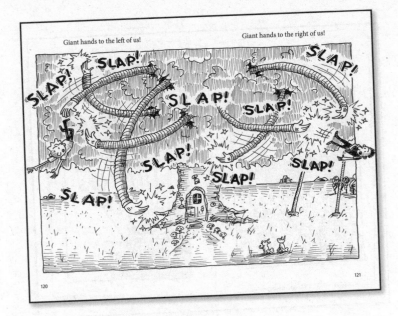

SLAP! SLAP! SLAP! SLAP! SLAP! SLAP! SLAP! SLAP! SLAP!

120

121

There are two dogs, a goat,
three horses, four goldfish, one cow,

two guinea pigs, one camel,
one donkey, thirteen flying cats

130

131

323

There's a blinding flash and then no more solar system.

"Oh, well, no use crying over un-invented solar systems," says Terry. "At least he didn't un-invent the whole universe."

"What a good idea!" says Professor Stupido. "Thank you so much, Terry! I'll get right on to it."

"You and your big mouth, Terry!" I say.

"Relax," he says. "As if he could even *do* that!"

Professor Stupido takes a deep breath.

Terry starts drawing all the animals on Earth.
    "Don't bother drawing all the rabbits," I say.
"Two will be enough."

"Why?" says Terry.
    "Don't worry," I say. "Just keep drawing. I'll tell you about the rabbits later."

304

305

"Well," says Terry, "what do you think?"
    "Action-packed!" I say. "It's got everything I asked for. The only thing missing is the explosion."
    "I can't wait to read it to the animals," says Jill. "They're going to love it—especially chapter seven!"

"It makes you wonder, though," I say. "Did everything we've just been through really happen or was it just a story made up by the machine?"
    "It sure *felt* real," says Terry. "Especially when Mr. Hee-Haw bit me on the hand."

327

"Well," says Terry, "what do you think?"

"Action-packed!" I say. "It's got everything I asked for. The only thing missing is the explosion."

"I can't wait to read it to the animals," says Jill. "They're going to love it—especially chapter seven!"

"It makes you wonder, though," I say. "Did everything we've just been through really happen or was it just a story made up by the machine?"

"It sure *felt* real," says Terry. "Especially when Mr. Hee-Haw bit me on the hand."

"Well, whether it was real or just a story," says Jill, "I expect you've both learned a *very* good lesson from all this."

"What?" says Terry.

"It's obvious, isn't it?" says Jill.

"Um . . ." says Terry. "Andy can't draw?"

"You already knew that," says Jill.

"He can't count?" says Terry.

"Obviously not," says Jill. "But that's not a moral."

"Look before you leap?" I say.

Jill sighs. "I think you'd both better read the book again," she says.

So we do.

"You know," says Terry when we're finished, "it seems to me that I invented the writing and drawing machine to save us work, but it ended up causing us much more trouble and bother than it would have been to just write the book ourselves in the first place."

"Well done, Terry!" says Jill. "That's the moral right there!"

"Ugh!" I say. "That stupid machine put a moral in and I *hate* stories with a moral!"

"Speaking of that stupid machine," says Terry, "where is it?"

We all look around.

"It's gone!" says Jill.

"Somebody must have stolen it while we were reading the book," says Terry.

"But who would *do* such a thing?" says Jill.

"*Them*, that's who!" I say, pointing to a group of fake postal workers making their way through the forest with our machine.

"Those postmen?" says Jill.

"They're *not* postmen," I say. "They're the Birthday Card Bandits! Now they'll be able to write stories just like ours . . . but with morals!"

"I thought you said you hated stories with morals?" says Jill.

"Yes, *I* do," I say, "but other people love that sort of stuff!"

"Relax, Andy," says Terry. "Remember the big-toe recognition security feature? If anyone other than us tries to start the machine, it will self-destruct."

We hear a loud explosion.

"Like that?" says Jill.

"*Exactly* like that!" says Terry. "Looks like you got your explosion after all, Andy!"

"Yeah," I say, "and even better, we're free of the Once-upon-a-time machine once and for all—it can't possibly redraw itself now!"

"Well, I think this calls for a special celebration," says Terry.

"Great idea!" I say. "What should we start with: marshmallows, lemonade, chocolate waterfall?"

"None of them," says Terry. "I've got something even better. Follow me!"

Jill and I follow Terry to the ice cream parlor. "Hot ice creams!" calls Edward Scooperhands excitedly. "Get your hot ice creams!"

"Hot ice cream?" I say. "But I thought Professor Stupido un-invented hot ice cream."

"He did," says Terry. "But when I was redrawing the universe I took the opportunity to redraw it and a few of the other things he had un-invented as well."

Jill chooses raspberry ripple, I choose rocky road and Terry orders three triple scoops of chocolate, double chocolate and triple chocolate.

"Wow!" says Jill. "Hot ice cream is delicious. It's just like cold ice cream, only *hot*!"

"Yeah," I say, "and no brain freeze!"

"Mmmm," says Terry. "Chocolatey!"

"Professor Stupido was crazy to un-invent this stuff," says Jill.

"Yeah," says Terry. "I'm starting to think that maybe he wasn't such a genius after all."

Terry gasps. "Oh no! Watch out for that frogpotamus, Andy!" he yells.

"What frogpotamus?" I say.

I look up to see a 10-ton frogpotamus hurtling toward me, its mouth wide open.

Everything goes dark.

And slimy.

And smelly.

This is even worse than being sneezed on by Terry!

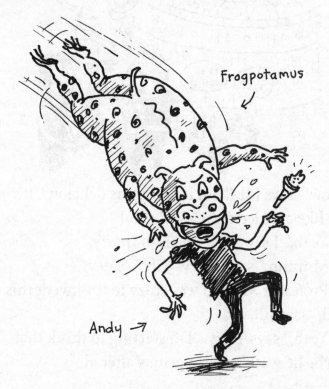

Frogpotamus

Andy →

"Be careful, Terry, don't hurt it!" I hear Jill saying as Terry pulls the frogpotamus off me.

"What about me?" I say.

"You'll be fine, Andy," says Jill. "But frogpotamuses are delicate and easily frightened!"

"Then why did it jump on my head?" I say.

"Because it wanted some of your ice cream," says Jill. "Frogpotamuses *love* hot ice cream. *Everybody* knows that."

"Well, *I* didn't," I say, wiping frogpotamus spit off my face with the handkerchief Terry drew me, "and I don't like frogpotamuses."

"Don't be mean," says Jill. "I think it's cute."

"You can have it if you want," says Terry.

"*Really?*" says Jill.

"Yes," I say. "From now on the treehouse is a frogpotamus-free zone."

"Thanks, Andy and Terry," says Jill. "See you both later."

She climbs onto the frogpotamus's back and whispers into its ear. It jumps out of the tree and hops off into the forest.

"So, that all worked out pretty well," says Terry. "Not only did we get to taste hot ice cream but Jill got a new pet frogpotamus and we got our book!"

"Yes," I say, "except that it's almost *five o'clock* and there's no way we're going to be able to get it to Mr. Big Nose on time!"

"Yes there is!" says Terry.

"How?"

"By *flying beetroot*, of course!" says Terry.

He whistles and two brand-new, shiny, flying beetroots whoosh up and hover in front of us.

"One for me . . . and one for you!" says Terry.

"Wow!" I say. "Thanks, Terry. But what about the vegetable vaporizer? Won't it vaporize them? Beetroots *are* vegetables, you know."

"No problem," says Terry. "When I redrew the vegetable vaporizer I added a flying beetroot-override switch."

"Brilliant, Terry!" I say. "Let's go! Up, up and away!"

339

"Will you tell me about the rabbits now, Andy?" says Terry.

"Sure," I say, "but first I want to talk about adding another 13 storys to the treehouse."

"You mean we're going to make a *52-story treehouse*?" says Terry.

"Yes," I say. "If that's what 39 plus 13 is."

"That's *exactly* what it is," says Terry. "And *then* you'll tell me about the rabbits?"

"Of course, Terry," I say. "I promise."

THE END

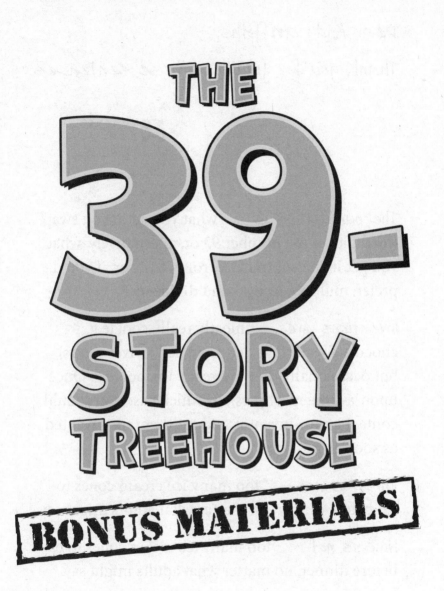

THE
39-
STORY
TREEHOUSE

BONUS MATERIALS

Dear Andy Griffiths,

Thank you for finishing these sentences.

xo,

SQUARE
FISH

The number 39 is . . . what you get if you swap the digits in the number 93 or, alternatively, what you get if you subtract 39 from 78 . . . or, if you'd prefer, multiply 39 by 3 and divide by 3.

Inventions are . . . mostly really cool (e.g. chocolate waterfalls, jet-propelled swivel chairs), but occasionally they are really uncool (e.g. Once-upon-a-time machines), in which case you should contact an un-inventor and get them un-invented as soon as possible.

Three is not . . . too many ice cream cones to eat before dinner, no matter what adults might say.

Nine is not . . . too many ice cream cones to eat before dinner, no matter what adults might say.

In 39 days, I will . . . be 39 days older, barring

any unfortunate accidents (i.e. falling into the tank full of man-eating sharks, falling into the volcano or getting scared to death on the world's scariest roller coaster).

3 + 9 = hippopotamus

Jill should . . . get her animals under control. They are even more badly behaved than Terry on a bad day.

I wish I could . . . travel across the universe at the speed of light on a flying beetroot. (Hey, I'm allowed to dream, aren't I?)

I'd like to give Terry . . . a flamethrower, except I would tell him it was a nostril-hair remover and he's so dumb, he'd probably believe it and end up setting his head on fire. That would be fun. (But that's just between you and me . . . please don't tell him I said that.)

Look! It's a . . . frogpotamus! Run! (Unless you want it to swallow your head, in which case, stay right where you are.)

I'd like to have a sleepover with . . . NONE OF JILL'S ANIMALS!!!

My 39 least favorite things are . . .
creepy little black spiders x 39.

Hey, why didn't you ask me about . . . the
time I broke the Guinness World Record for the
largest gathering of people dressed as trees at
Ellenbrook Primary School in Perth, Western
Australia, on September 10, 2014?

Dear Terry Denton,
Thank you for finishing these sentences.

XO,

SQUARE
FISH

The number 39 is . . . how many times I hit Andy with a giant pink plastic flamingo. He deserved it, I tell you.

Inventions are . . . un-invented by un-inventors.

Three is not . . . a crowd. Seven billion is a crowd.

Nine is not . . . a chicken.

In 39 days, I will . . . hatch my very own chicken.

3 + 9 = that's a hard one, because I think it is not 13. And I only know things that add up to 13.

Jill should . . . and Terry and Andy shouldn't.

I wish I could . . . take my cow through the car wash.

I'd like to give Andy . . . my cold, especially my sniffly nose.

Look! It's a . . . clean cow! She DID go through the car wash!

I'd like to have a sleepover with . . . my 39 penguin friends . . . in the fridge.

My 39 least favorite things are . . . raindrops on roses, whiskers on kittens, and 37 tap-dancing donkeys called Mr. Hee-Haw.

Hey, why didn't you ask me about . . . my giant pink plastic flamingo?

The treehouse just keeps on expanding!
Come see a make-your-own pizza parlor, a Ninja
Snail Training Academy, and a high-tech
detective agency!

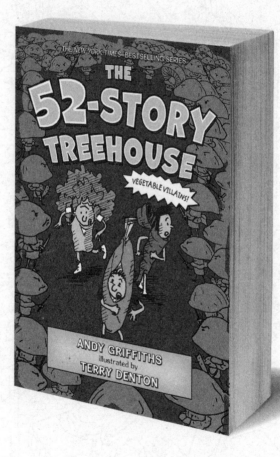

Read on for a sneak peek.

We've added a watermelon-smashing room,

a chainsaw-juggling level,

a make-your-own-pizza parlor,

a rocket-powered carrot-launcher,

a giant hair dryer that is so strong it practically blasts the hair right off your head. . . .

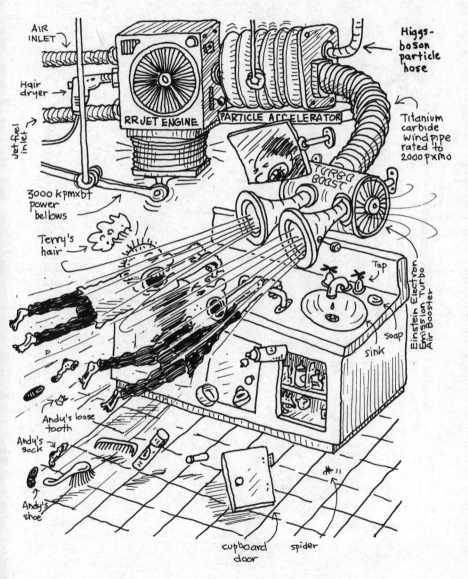